Other Kipper books

Kipper
Kipper's Toybox
Kipper's Birthday
Kipper's Snowy Day
Where, Oh Where, is Kipper's Bear?
Kipper's Book of Colours
Kipper's Book of Opposites
Kipper's Book of Counting
Kipper's Book of Weather

First published 1999
by Hodder Children's Books,
a division of Hodder Headline plc,
338 Euston Road, London NW1 3BH

This hardback edition published 2000

10 9 8

ISBN 0 340 799269

A catalogue record for this book
is available from the British Library.
The right of Mick Inkpen to be identitfied
as the author of this work
has been asserted by him.

Sandcastle

Mick Inkpen

*Hodder
Children's
Books*

A division of Hodder Headline

K ipper was making
sandcastles.
It wasn't easy.
The first one wobbled
and fell over. The second
one crumbled at the corner.
But the third one
was just right.

Kipper made a big
pile of sand and
patted it smooth.
Then he dug,
and piled, and patted
some more. And this is
what he made.

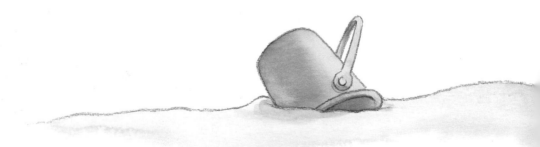

A seagull landed on
Kipper's castle.
It squawked and flew
away again.
'That's what I need!'
said Kipper.
'Something to
go on top!'

Kipper found some
seaweed and some
pebbles.

'No, they won't do,'
he said.

He found a shell.
It was pink and pointy.

'Perfect!' he said.

Kipper put the pink and pointy shell on his castle.

But the pink and pointy shell got up and walked away . . .

. . .there was a little crab inside!

So Kipper stopped
building his sandcastle.
He bought himself an
ice cream, and a sticky
lolly too!

While he was licking
the last bit of lolly,
an idea
popped into
his head.